Estimados padres de familia,

Están a punto de comenzar una emocionante aventura con su hijo y nosotros ¡seremos su guía!

Su misión es: Convertir a su hijo en un lector.

Nuestra misión: Hacerlo divertido.

LEVEL UP! READERS les da oportunidades para lectura independiente para todos los niños, comenzando con aquellos que ya saben el abecedario. Nuestro programa tiene una estructura flexible que hará que los nuevos lectores se sientan emocionados y que alcancen sus logros, no aburridos o frustrados. Los Niveles de Lectura Guiada en la parte posterior de cada libro serán su guía para encontrar el nivel adecuado. ¿Cómo comenzar?

Cada nivel de lectura desarrolla nuevas habilidades:

Nivel 1: PREPARANDO: Desde conocer el abecedario hasta decifrar palabras.
lenguaje básico – repetición – claves visuales
Niveles de Lectura Guiada: aa, A, B, C, D

Nivel 2: MEJORANDO: Desde descifrar palabras individuales hasta leer oraciones completas.
palabras comunes – oraciones cortas – cuentos sencillos
Niveles de Lectura Guiada: C, D, E, F, G

Nivel 3: A JUGAR: Desde leer oraciones sencillas hasta disfrutar cuentos completos.
nuevas palabras – temas comunes – historias divertidas
Niveles de Lectura Guiada: F, G, H, I, J, K

Nivel 4: EL RETO: Navega por oraciones complejas y aprende nuevo vocabulario.
vocabulario interesante – oraciones más largas – cuentos emocionantes
Niveles de Lectura Guiada: H, I, J, K, L, M

Nivel 5: EXPLORA: Prepárate para leer libros en capítulos.
capítulos cortos – párrafos – historias complejas
Niveles de Lectura Guiada: K, L, M, N, O, P

¡Dele el control al lector!

Aventuras y diversión le esparan en cada nivel.

Obtenga más información en:
littlebeebooks.com/levelupreaders

Dear Parents,

W9-AWG-080

Your mission: Raise a reader.

Our mission: Make it fun.

LEVEL UP! READERS provides independent reading opportunities for all children, starting with those who already know the alphabet. Our program's flexible structure helps new readers feel excited and accomplished, not bored or frustrated. The Guided Reading Level shown on the back of each book helps caregivers and educators find just the right fit. So where do you start?

Each level unlocks new skills:

Level 1: GET READY: From knowing the alphabet to decoding words.
basic language – repetition – picture clues
Guided Reading Levels: aa, A, B, C, D

Level 2: POWER UP: From decoding single words to reading whole sentences.
common words – short sentences – simple stories
Guided Reading Levels: C, D, E, F, G

Level 3: PLAY: From reading simple sentences to enjoying whole stories.
new words – popular themes – fun stories
Guided Reading Levels: F, G, H, I, J, K

Level 4: CHALLENGE: Navigate complex sentences and learn new vocabulary.
interest-based vocabulary – longer sentences – exciting stories
Guided Reading Levels: H, I, J, K, L, M

Level 5: EXPLORE: Prepare for chapter books.
short chapters – paragraphs – complex stories
Guided Reading Levels: K, L, M, N, O, P

Put the controls in the hands of the reader!

Fun and adventure await on every level.

Find out more at:
littlebeebooks.com/levelupreaders

BuzzPop

An imprint of Little Bee Books
251 Park Avenue South, New York, NY 10010
Copyright © 2019 Disney Enterprises, Inc.
All rights reserved, including the right of reproduction
in whole or in part in any form.
BuzzPop and associated colophon are trademarks
of Little Bee Books.

Manufactured in the United States of America LAK 0919
For more information about special discounts on bulk purchases,
please contact Little Bee Books at sales@littlebeebooks.com.

First Edition

ISBN 978-1-4998-0877-3 (pbk)
10 9 8 7 6 5 4 3 2 1
ISBN 978-1-4998-0878-0 (hc)
10 9 8 7 6 5 4 3 2 1

buzzpopbooks.com

Living Fossils

by Andrew Whitmore

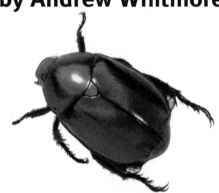

Table of Contents

Chapter 1
Animals That Time Forgot............2

Chapter 2
Undersea Survivors..................4

Chapter 3
Ancient Insects......................8

Chapter 4
Outlasting the Dinosaurs...........10

Chapter 5
Future Fossils.....................14

Glossary/Index...................15

Comprehension Check...............16

Chapter 1
Animals That Time Forgot

Most kinds of animals that lived a long time ago are no longer living. Scientists think that 99.9 percent of all **species** that have ever lived are now **extinct**. Some animals died because they were unable to **adapt** to changes in the world. Others died in earthquakes and floods.

But there are some species that have survived for millions of years and have not changed much. Some people call them "living **fossils**." Like real fossils, living fossils can help us learn about the past.

◑ A real fossil is viewed under a magnifying glass.

🎧 Coelacanths were thought to be extinct. Then one was caught in 1938.

One example of a living fossil is a coelacanth (*SEE-luh-kanth*). This ancient fish still lives in the Indian Ocean. It looks the same as real fossils of coelacanths that are 400 million years old.

How Real Fossils Form

1. An animal or insect dies.

2. The dead animal or insect is buried.

3. Soft parts of the body break down.

4. Earth hardens around the body to form rock.

5. The skeleton's outine is a fossil.

Chapter 2
Undersea Survivors

Sharks have lived in the sea for more than 350 million years. They are very good hunters. They use their nostrils to smell, but not to breathe. They breathe through their gills.

Sharks can have up to 3,000 teeth. Fossil shark teeth are very similar to those found in sharks today. The food they eat and their way of hunting have not changed much over time.

↻ A great white shark may not eat for up to two months after a big meal.

A Giant Ancient Shark

The megalodon (*MEG-uh-luh-dahn*) was a giant meat-eating shark. It lived between 25 million and 1.6 million years ago. It was more than 40 feet (12 meters) long. Each tooth was the size of a person's hand. It ate mostly whales. The megalodon's jaws could open wide to swallow huge fish.

Dr. Jeremiah Clifford holds the jaws of a great white shark. He stands in a model of a megalodon's jaws. ➲

Great white sharks can grow up to 23 feet (7 meters) long. That's about the size of a moving van. In the past, some sharks were even bigger.

No one knows for sure how long a great white shark can live. Some scientists think one can live as long as 100 years.

◉ The leatherback is the world's largest sea turtle. It weighs more than 1,000 pounds (454 kilograms).

Turtles have also been around for a long time. Their thick shells have helped them to **survive**. When one is attacked, it can pull its head, tail, and legs inside. This keeps them safe from other animals.

The first turtles lived more than 100 million years ago. This was around the time of the first dinosaurs. The turtles lived in warm seas. The seas covered what is now part of Europe and North America.

Horseshoe crabs have not changed much in 430 million years. This may be because other animals do not like to eat them. Their bodies are protected by strong, leathery shells.

Horseshoe crabs aren't really crabs. They are related to spiders and scorpions.

The horseshoe crab has a small body under its shell. There is very little meat for other animals to eat. ↻

Chapter 3
Ancient Insects

Many insects have not changed much since ancient times.

The emperor dragonfly has stayed the same for 230 million years. Fossils of dragonflies have been found in ancient rocks. The fossils confirm that these creatures were the same as those still flying around today.

Dragonflies are very good hunters. They can easily catch and eat other insects. They grab them right out of the air.

Most birds are unable to catch dragonflies. A dragonfly's four wings help it fly faster than most birds and insects.

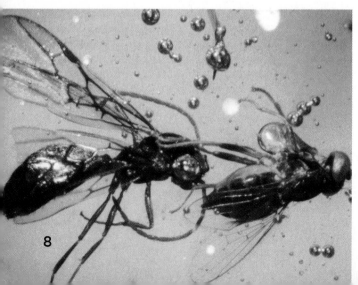

☾ These dragonflies were trapped in sticky plant sap millions of years ago.

This scarab beetle looks the same as scarab beetles did millions of years ago. ⮑

The earliest beetle fossils are 230 million years old. Beetles have not changed much since they first appeared on Earth.

Beetles are the most common form of insect alive today. They can live in many different temperatures. The hard covering on their wings protects them from many insects and animals.

Chapter 4
Outlasting the Dinosaurs

Crocodiles look a lot like dinosaurs. They are closely related. But crocodiles have outlived the dinosaurs by about 65 million years.

Crocodiles are very tough. They can hold their breath under water for up to two hours. They can go without food for up to a year.

↻ A crocodile's body is protected by a bony covering.

⬆ This illustration shows sea life 65 million years ago.
A crocodile was the biggest animal in the sea.

The largest living crocodiles grow to
be about 26 feet (8 meters) long. A
long time ago, some crocodiles grew
to be twice this size. They would have
been about the size of a school bus!
These huge crocodiles probably attacked
dinosaurs as they came to the river
to drink.

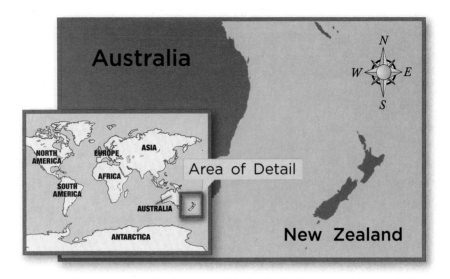

🎧 Tuataras were once found all over New Zealand. They were hunted and killed by animals brought by settlers.

Tuataras (*TOO-uh-TAH-ruhz*) look like big lizards. But they are the only survivors of a group of **reptiles** that lived 250 million to 70 million years ago. Today they can only be found on a few islands near New Zealand.

Tuataras seem to live their whole lives in slow motion. They only need to breathe around once every hour. Their eggs take between 11 and 16 months to hatch. The young tuataras grow very slowly. Maybe this is why they can live to be more than 100 years old.

A tuatara has a third eye on top of its head between its other eyes. This eye can't be used for seeing, but it reacts to light. Scientists believe it may help the tuatara decide if it has been in the sun too long.

Tuataras live in burrows. They only come out to eat at night.

The tuatara gets its name from the row of large spines along its neck, back, and tail. *Tuatara* means "peaks on the back" in the native Maori language. ⟳

Chapter 5
Future Fossils

There are valid reasons to believe we may find even more "living fossils" in the future. Some parts of the world have not yet been fully explored. Many people are hopeful that learning about these animals will help us learn more about the history of life on Earth.

This chart shows that all of the animals and insects in this book lived long before humans. ↻

Time Line of Life on Earth

Years Ago	First Creatures Lived
430 million ←●→	horseshoe crabs
400 million ←●→	coelacanth
350 million ←●→	sharks
250 million ←●→	tuataras
230 million ←●→	dragonflies/beetles
220 million ←●→	dinosaurs
200 million ←●→	crocodiles
100 million ←●→	turtles
65 million ←●→	dinosaurs disappear
Less than 1 million ←●→	humans

Glossary

adapt *(uh-DAPT)* to change to suit different conditions *(page 2)*

extinct *(ek-STINGT)* no longer living *(page 2)*

fossils *(FOS-uhlz)* the remains of plants or animals of a past age preserved in earth or rock *(page 2)*

reptiles *(REP-tyuhls)* cold-blooded animals that breathe air, usually lay eggs, and have skin covered with scales or bony plates *(page 12)*

species *(SPEE-sheez)* a group of animals or plants that have many things in common *(page 2)*

survive *(suhr-VIVE)* to live through *(page 6)*

Index

beetles, *9, 14*

coelacanths, *3, 14*

crocodiles, *10-11, 14*

dragonflies, *8, 14*

fossils (real), *2-3, 8-9*

great white shark, *4-5*

horseshoe crabs, *7, 14*

insects, *8-9*

megalodon, *5*

sharks, *4-5, 14*

tuataras, *12-14*

turtles, *6, 14*

Comprehension Check

Retell

Use the photos to help you retell the information in this book.

Think and Compare

1. Turn to page 8. Why are dragonflies very good hunters? *(Summarize)*

2. Some rainforests and underwater areas have still not been explored. Would you like to explore new places to look for more living fossils? Explain your answer. *(Apply)*

3. Why do you think scientists look for and study fossils? *(Analyze)*

Literacy Activities

WRITE ABOUT IT

Animal Description

Write a description of your favorite animal in this book. Tell how it lives and how it defends itself from animals that attack it.

SCIENCE CONNECTION

Make a Summary Poster

Reread pages 12 and 13. Make a poster about the tuatara. Tell about how the animal lives. Draw pictures to explain your writing. Make people want to learn more about this "living fossil."

B

Living Fossils

Some kinds of animals have been on Earth since the dinosaurs lived. Find out how they live today.

2.3 Week 3

The **McGraw·Hill** Companies

ISBN 0-02-192597-6

99701

9 780021 925971

2

Mc Graw Hill **Macmillan McGraw-Hill**

Disney

FROZEN II

Un viaje juntos y separados
Journey Together and Apart

Adaptation by R. J. Cregg
Translation by Laura Collado Píriz
Illustrated by the Disney Storybook Art Team

BuzzPop

Anna y Elsa eran **niñas pequeñas**.
Anna and Elsa were **little kids**.

Ahora ellas son **adultas**.
Now they are **grown-ups**.

Elsa está **confiada**.
Elsa is **confident**.

Anna está **preocupada**.
Anna is **worried**.

La calle está **abarrotada**.
The street is **crowded**.

La fuente está **vacía**.

The fountain is **empty**.

Anna, Elsa, Olaf, Kristoff y Sven
viajan a lo **alto** de la montaña.
Anna, Elsa, Olaf, Kristoff, and Sven
travel **high** up the mountain.

Ellos viajan por una llanura **baja**.
They travel across the **low** plain.

Ellos **entran** en una niebla mágica.
They **go into** the magic mist.

Ellos **salen** al bosque encantado.
They **come out** in the Enchanted Forest.

Primero, Olaf, está **asustado**.
First, Olaf is **frightened**.

Luego, él está **emocionado**.
Then, he is **excited**.

Un viento mágico obliga a Anna, Elsa, Olaf, Kristoff y Sven a **separarse**.

A magical wind forces Anna, Elsa, Olaf, Kristoff, and Sven **apart**.

Pero unos extraños los **unen**.
Strangers bring them **together**.

Elsa hace **hielo**.
Elsa makes **ice**.

Un espíritu mágico hace **fuego**.
A magical spirit makes **fire**.

Elsa pone **contento** al espíritu.
Elsa makes the spirit **happy**.

Pero Olaf, Anna y Elsa descubren
algo **triste**.

But Olaf, Anna, and Elsa discover
something **sad**.

Anna y Elsa se **reúnen**.
Anna and Elsa are **united**.

Pero ellas tienen que **separarse**.
But they must **separate**.

Anna y Olaf flotan sobre
las aguas **tranquilas**.
Anna and Olaf float over
calm water.

Elsa corre por unas aguas **embravecidas**.
Elsa runs across **rough** water.

El espíritu agua es **fuerte**.
The Water Spirit is **strong**.

Elsa es **gentil**.
Elsa is **gentle**.

Elsa encuentra el camino ella **sola**.
Elsa finds her way **on her own**.

Anna y Olaf encuentran su camino **juntos**.

Anna and Olaf find their way **together**.

Para estos amigos, el **final**
no es más que el **principio**.
For these friends, the **end**
is just the **beginning**.

¿Te diste cuenta?

En español decimos:
Elsa <u>está</u> confiada.
Usamos "**<u>está</u>**" para describir cómo sesiente Elsa.
Elsa <u>es</u> gentil.
Usamos "**<u>es</u>**" para describir las características de Elsa o cómo es.

En inglés, decimos:
Elsa <u>is</u> confident.
Elsa <u>is</u> gentle.
Usamos "<u>is</u>" para describir cómo sesiente Elsa y cómo es.

¿Qué más puedes usar para describir a Elsa?

Did you notice?

In Spanish, we say:
Elsa <u>está</u> confiada.
We use "**<u>está</u>**" to describe how Elsa is feeling.
Elsa <u>es</u> gentil.
We use "**<u>es</u>**" to describe Elsa's characteristics, or what she is like.

In English, we say:
Elsa <u>is</u> confident.
Elsa <u>is</u> gentle.
We use "<u>is</u>" to describe how Elsa is feeling and what Elsa is like.

How else can you describe Elsa?

Glosario   Glossary

confiado/a describe a alguien que se está seguro de sus habilidades
confident describes someone who feels good about their abilities

abarrotado/a describe algo lleno de demasiada gente o cosas
crowded describes something filled with too many people or things

vacío/a describe algo que no tiene nada dentro
empty describes something with nothing inside

un extraño es una persona a la que no conoces
a stranger is someone you do not know

separado/a describe a personas o cosas que están a cierta distancia unas de otras
separate describes people or things that are detached or on their own

tranquilo/a describe a una persona o a una cosa que está calmada o sosegada
calm describes a person or thing that is quiet or settled

¿Qué otras palabras nuevas aprendiste?
What other new words did you learn?